To Tom and Adelaide Ryan, and their brood—Ryan, Amy,
Brendan, Kira, Celia, Nicholas, Shelby, Devin and little Mya.

Library and Archives Canada Cataloguing in Publication

Beck, Andrea, 1956-
Pierre's friends / written and illustrated by Andrea Beck.

Also available in an electronic format.
ISBN 978-1-55469-030-5

I. Title.
PS8553.E2948P45 2010   jC813'.54   C2010-903516-X

Summary: Pierre, a pampered poodle, is lonely, so he sets out
to find his friends and bring them home.

First published in the United States, 2010
Library of Congress Control Number: 2010928737

Mixed Sources
Cert no. SW-COC-001271
© 1996 FSC

*Orca Book Publishers is dedicated to preserving the environment
and has printed this book on paper certified by the
Forest Stewardship Council.*

Orca Book Publishers gratefully acknowledges the support for
its publishing programs provided by the following agencies:
the Government of Canada through the Canada Book Fund and the
Canada Council for the Arts, and the Province of British Columbia
through the BC Arts Council and the Book Publishing Tax Credit.

Cover and interior artwork by Andrea Beck
Design by Teresa Bubela

ORCA BOOK PUBLISHERS
PO Box 5626, STN. B
VICTORIA, BC CANADA
V8R 6S4

ORCA BOOK PUBLISHERS
PO Box 468
CUSTER, WA USA
98240-0468

www.orcabook.com
Printed and bound in Canada.

13 12 11 10 • 4 3 2 1

Pierre's Friends

written and illustrated by ANDREA BECK

ORCA BOOK PUBLISHERS

Pierre Le Poof was a pampered pooch. He had almost everything a dog could want—a full dish, a soft pillow and Miss Murphy, the person he adored.

But Pierre missed his friends, Sparky and Lou.

As he sat in his window overlooking the park, Pierre decided to go find them.

Sparky and Lou liked to wrestle and play.
They liked to dig holes and sniff dirt.
Sparky and Lou were fun! But they lived
in a park on the other side of town, and
Pierre didn't know how to get there.
He needed a plan.

Miss Murphy said the park outside his window stretched right across the city.

That's where he would begin.

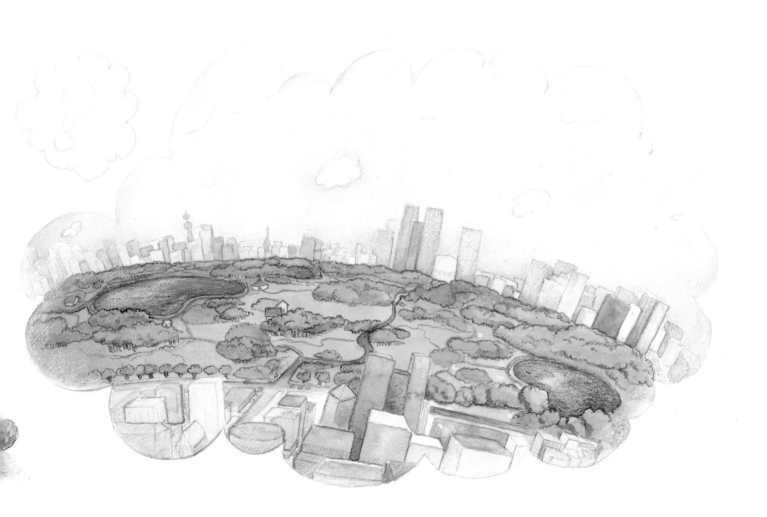

Pierre figured Miss Murphy wouldn't mind if he brought Sparky and Lou home. She always said dogs and people belonged together. Miss Murphy even said grumpy old Mr. Farnham next door wasn't really grumpy. He was just lonely because years ago he had lost his dog.

"He needs a little buddy," she told Pierre.

Surely that meant Miss Murphy had room in her heart for another little buddy, or two?

Pierre's plan was simple.

Miss Murphy always watched her favorite TV show at two in the afternoon and had a snooze afterward. He would slip out the fire-escape window, run over to the park, find Sparky and Lou and bring them back before she woke up.

It's a good plan, thought Pierre.

The next day, Pierre was ready.

At two o'clock, Miss Murphy turned on the TV. Pierre snuck out the window, down the fire escape and over to the park.

"Where are Sparky and Lou?" he asked every dog he met.

"Old Wheezer will know," said a helpful mutt.

"He lives under the stone bridge."

Pierre found Old Wheezer licking an empty chip bag.

"Where can I find Sparky and Lou?" Pierre asked. "I want to bring them home with me."

Old Wheezer's tail thumped.

"Home?" he said softly. "I had a home once." Then he nodded toward a path. "Follow that trail, pup. You'll find your friends."

Pierre thanked Old Wheezer, but he had run out of time. He rushed home and was back beside Miss Murphy just as she opened her eyes.

That evening Pierre's tail wagged at every thought of Sparky and Lou. Yet when Miss Murphy filled his bowl with his favorite stew, it was thin Old Wheezer he remembered.

The following day at two o'clock, Pierre snuck out again. He sped through the park and along the trail. At the end of the path he spotted his friends.

"Pierre!" howled Sparky.

"We knew you'd come back," said Lou.

They bounded over to Pierre, and after a good tussle he invited them home.

Pierre's friends looked at him.

"Why would we leave the park?" Lou asked.

"You'll have a comfy bed," said Pierre. "You'll be warm and dry, and Miss Murphy will feed you every day."

"Every day?" asked Lou.

"Whoohooo!" cheered Sparky. "Let's go!"

They followed Pierre across the park, up the fire escape and in through the window.

Once inside, Pierre hesitated. Miss Murphy loved dogs, but two strays from the park might be a surprise.

Pierre was right.

"Ahhh!" shrieked Miss Murphy.

Pierre nuzzled Sparky, then Lou. He wagged the tip of his tail.

Miss Murphy sighed. "Okay, your friends can stay until I find them a home."

FOUND

Miss Murphy gave Sparky and Lou a bath. Then, to Pierre's dismay, she made a poster and left the apartment.

She came back smiling.

"Mrs. Ford is looking for a dog, maybe two. She's coming to meet your friends tomorrow," she said.

Pierre's heart soared.

Mrs. Ford lived two windows over on the fire escape. He could play with Sparky and Lou anytime!

Pierre was happy about Sparky and Lou, but that night, he lay wide awake. He tossed and turned and turned and tossed. Finally he got up, found a leash and crept out the fire-escape window.

He had one thing left to do.

Pierre ran through the dark to the old stone bridge.

"Wheezer," he whispered. He looped the leash around Wheezer's neck and tied a perfect knot.

"What are you up to, pup?" asked the old dog.

"Now you look like someone's little buddy," said Pierre.

"Someone's buddy?" Wheezer shook himself awake. Then, with a jaunty step, he followed Pierre back to his building and all the way to Mr. Farnham's door.

Pierre jumped up and rang the buzzer.

The door opened.

"What time is it?" growled Mr. Farnham.

Old Wheezer's tail beat so fast it looked as if he might lift off. Then Pierre saw something he'd never seen before—Mr. Farnham smiled.

"Who might you be, old pal?" he asked gently. "You sure could use a meal."

He knelt down and Old Wheezer leapt into his arms.

Pierre slipped away.

Back home, Pierre curled up on his comfy cushion
and sighed a happy sigh.

Now he had everything a dog could want.

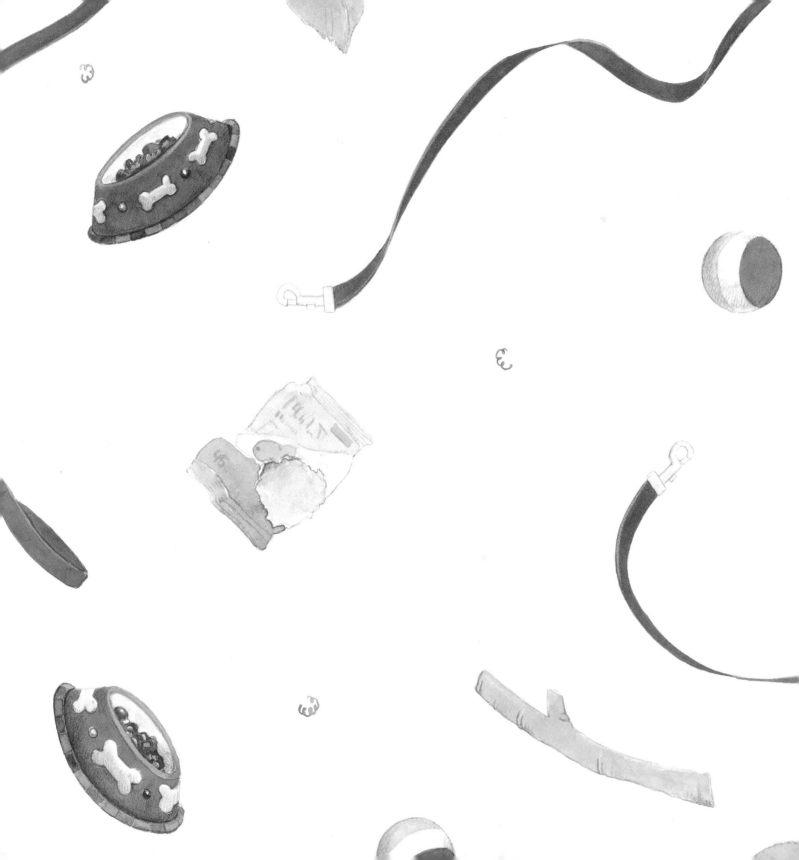

Goodnight Cajun Land

WRITTEN BY CORNELL P. LANDRY

ILLUSTRATED BY SEAN GAUTREAUX

ISBN 978-0-9846710-6-9

10 9 8 7 6 5 4 3 2 1

Design:
Sean Gautreaux
mardigras@yahoo.com
www.Art504.com

Published by:
Black Pot Publishing
P.O. Box 35
Gretna, Louisiana 70054
www.BlackPotPublishing.com
www.CornellPLandry.com
www.CornellLandry.com

For general information or to contact the author about school readings and signings, email
info@blackpotpublishing.com

Printed in Canada

I dedicate this book to my "Biggest Fan," Les Schouest.
I met Les when he was in prekindergarten. His teacher told me that I had to meet this little boy who carried around a copy of **Goodnight Nola** wherever he went. Since our introduction Les and I have remained in contact over the years. I try to visit him any time I am in Lafayette, Louisiana. During one of my visits with Les, he read me a poem that he had written about the UL Ragin Cajuns. When he finished the poem, he asked me if I was ever going to make a book about Lafayette, like **Goodnight Nola**. I gave some thought to the idea, and I came up with **Goodnight Cajun Land**. Thank you, Les, for being my inspiration for this book and for continuing to be my buddy.

A very special thanks goes out to my "Cajun Connection," Michelle Alcantar Fonseca, Betsy Bradford Lopez, and Mike & Tanya Blondiau. They constantly fed me ideas of what needed to be included in this book. Thank you all.

Last, but definitely not least, to my children Bailey, Corinne, and Cooper. My world revolves around the three of you. Love you to the Moon and back.

Goodnight seafood gumbo
Goodnight etouffee

Bon nuit mes amies
Laissez le bon temps rouler

Goodnight boudin and cracklin's
And specialty meats
Goodnight boucheries
That make all these great treats

Goodnight to Best Stop
Goodnight to Don's
Goodnight to Landry's
Goodnight to Prejean's

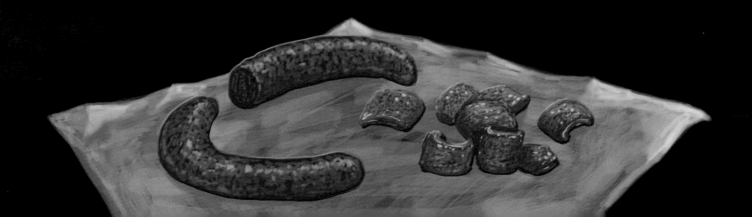

Goodnight cayenne peppers
All shades of red

To Tabasco hot sauce
and Evangeline Maid bread

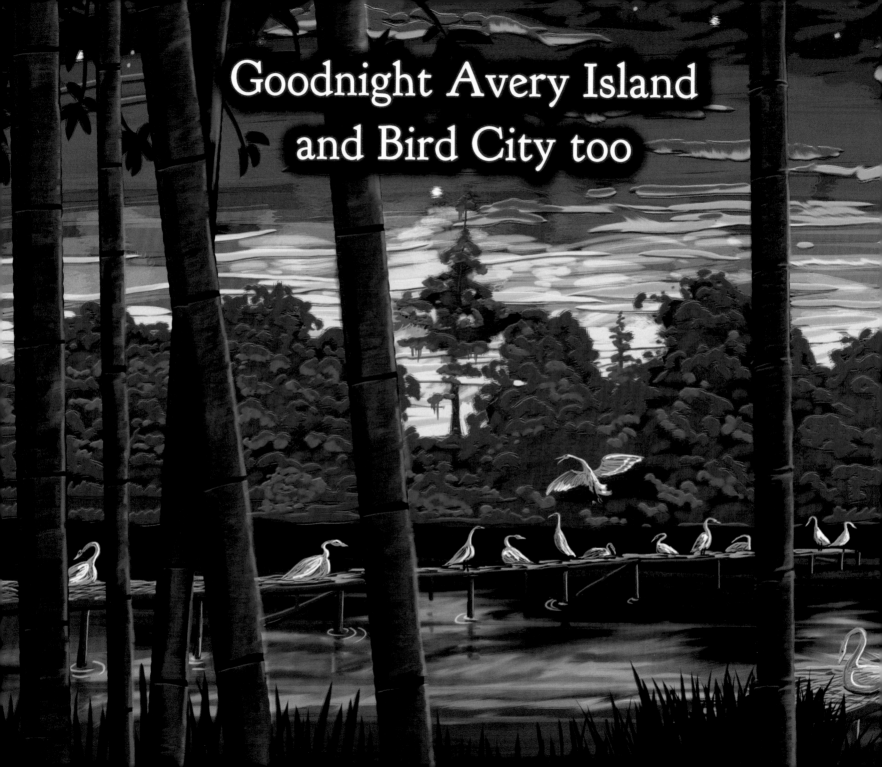

Goodnight Avery Island
and Bird City too

To the snowy egrets
and towering bamboo

Goodnight red and white
Yelling "Ah-Yee"
Hustle and bustle
Fight for victory

Goodnight Cajun dancers
All full of pep

As they sashay and waltz
and dance the two step

Goodnight Mr. Longfellow
All the images you evoke
In your poem about Cajuns
And the Evangeline Oak

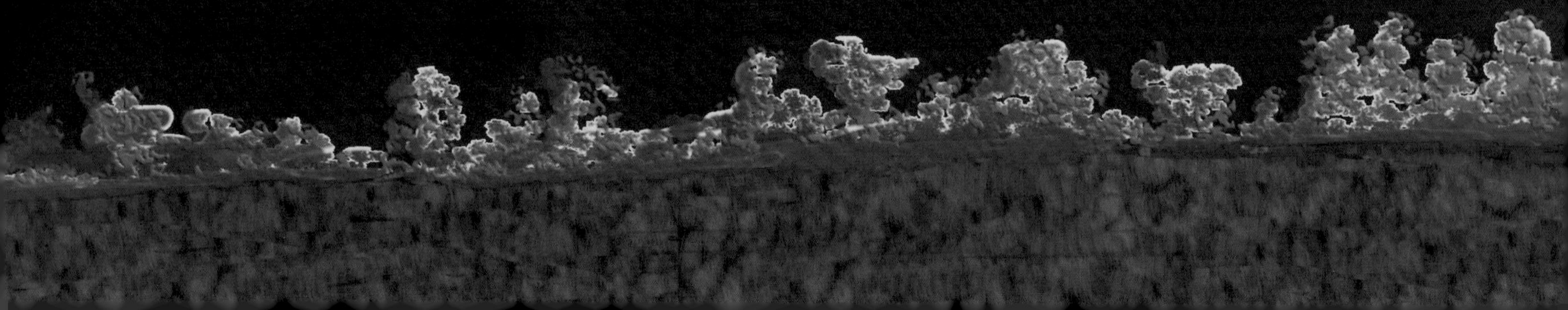

Goodnight Acadian Village

And the frogs in Rayne too

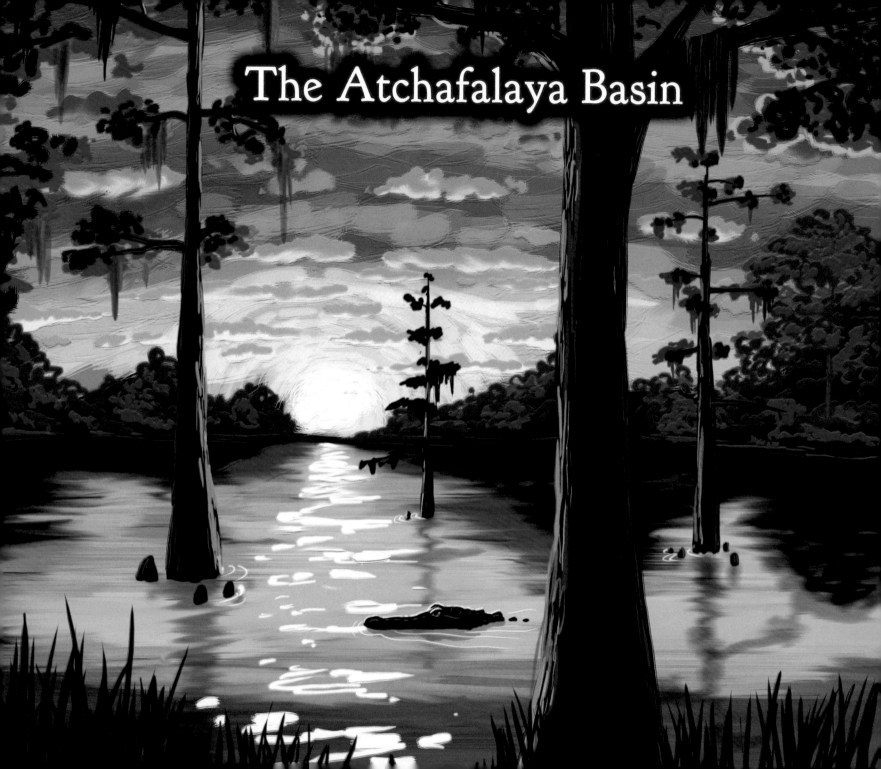

The Atchafalaya Basin

Breaux Bridge and Mamou

Bon nuit Acadiana
Little towns, yet so grand
Goodnight to you all
Throughout Cajun Land

Welcome to Louisiana

Bienvenue en Louisiane

Fais do do bebe boys
Fais do do bebe girls

Fais do do cher bebes
All over the world

ACKNOWLEDGMENTS (as they appear in book)

<u>Gumbo and Etouffee</u> - Two key dishes in cajun cuisine. Gumbo is the African word for okra. Etouffee means to smother.

<u>Bon Nuit Mes Amies</u> - Good Night my friends

<u>Laissez Le Bon Temps Rouler</u> - Let the good times roll

<u>Boudin and Cracklin</u> - Boudin is a meat based rice dressing that is stuffed into hog casing. Links of boudin are usually poached, but can also be smoked or grilled. Cracklins are crispy browned pieces of pig fat.

<u>Boucherie</u> - A butcher shop. Also, a harvesting of a pig into all different cuts of meat.

<u>Best Stop Super Market</u> - Opened in Scott, La in 1986. One of Acadiana's favorite meat markets.

<u>Don's</u> - A specialty meat store that opened in Carencro, La in 1993. Always a voter favorite.

<u>Landry's</u> - "From the time the doors opened in 1947 at the first location in Lafayette, Louisiana, out of a family's home, to the present day, Landry's Seafood has developed a nationwide reputation for delivering an unmatched dining experience for its guests."

<u>Prejean's</u> - In 1980 was named "the world's first cajun themed restaurant".

<u>Tabasco hot sauce</u> - World famous hot sauce, created by Edmund McIlhenny in the 1860's, on Avery Island, La.

<u>Evangeline Maid Bread</u> - Making quality bread in Acadiana since 1919.

<u>Bird City</u> - A bird sanctuary located on Avery Island La. It was founded by E.A. McIlhenny in the 1890's. Snowywhite egrets and other water birds return to the sanctuary each year.

<u>Ragin Cajuns / "The Swamp"</u> - The Ragin Cajuns represent the University of Louisiana at Lafayette. Football games are played in Cajun Field which is nicknamed "The Swamp".

<u>Chank-a-Chank/Frottoir/Zydeco</u> - Zydeco music is cajun music thats given its distinctive sound by use of the accordion, fiddle, and the frottoir (wash board). It is sometimes called "Chank-a-Chank" music because of the sound the forks make as they go up and down the washboard. The word Zydeco is said to come from a contraction of the song "Les haricots sont pas sale", which translates as "The snap beans aren't salty".

<u>Colinda/Ti-na-na/Jolie Blonde</u> - are three very popular songs in cajun music. Jolie Blonde is considered "the cajun national anthem".

<u>Evangeline Oak</u> - Longfellow's poem "Evangeline" immortalized the tragedy of the Acadian exile from Nova Scotia in 1755. This oak marks the legendary meeting place of Emmeline Labiche and Louis Arceneaux, the counterparts of Evangeline and Gabriel. (this is taken from the plaque which stands in front of the Evangeline Oak)

<u>Acadiana/Acadian Village</u> - Acadiana is the home of the "cajun people" or Acadians, who settled in southwest Louisiana after their expulsion from Nova Scotia in 1755. The Acadian Village in Lafayette La represents cajun living in the 1800's

<u>Rayne/Breaux Bridge/Mamou</u> - Rayne La is known as the "Frog Capital of the World". Breaux Bridge and Mamou are two cities in Acadiana.

<u>Fais Do Do</u> - is short for "Fais Dormir" which translates to "Make Sleep". Cajun tradition states that families would get together at someones house and have a "Bal de maison" or "house party". Before mothers could actually take place in the dance festivities, they would have to put the babies to sleep. Mothers would be heard saying "Fais Do-Do Cher Bebe" or "make sleep dear baby".

Check out these other titles
by Cornell P. Landry

Goodnight NOLA

Happy Mardi Gras

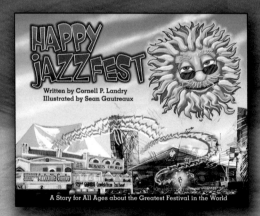

Happy Jazzfest

One Dat, Two Dat,
Are You A Who Dat?

Le Petit Bonhomme Janvier

The Amazing Adventure of
Mardi Gras Bead Dog

Monte the Lion

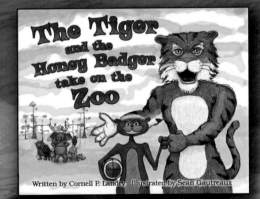

The Tiger and the Honey
Badger Take on the Zoo

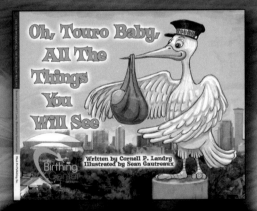

Oh, Touro Baby, All The
Things You Will See